Wicked Baba Yaga

GH00865266

Written by Sarah Shillam

Illustrated by Tomislav Zlatic

Anya's Escape 3

Enchanted Water 18

Published by Pearson Education Limited, Edinburgh Gate, Harlow, Essex, CM20 2JE.

www.pearsonschools.co.uk

Text © Pearson Education Limited 2013

Designed by Georgia Styring
Original illustrations © Tomislav Zlatic 2013
Illustrated by Tomislav Zlatic, Sylvie Poggio Artists Agency

The right of Sarah Shillam to be identified as author of this work has been asserted
by her in accordance with the Copyright, Designs and Patents Act 1988.

First published 2013

17 16 15 14 13
10 9 8 7 6 5 4 3 2 1

British Library Cataloguing in Publication Data
A catalogue record for this book is available from the British Library

ISBN 978 0 435 14438 8

Printed and bound in Dubai by Oriental Press.

Acknowledgements
We would like to thank Bangor Central Integrated Primary School, Northern Ireland;
Bishop Henderson Church of England Primary School, Somerset; Bletchingdon
Parochial Church of England Primary School, Oxfordshire; Brookside Community
Primary School, Somerset; Bude Park Primary School, Hull; Carisbrooke Church
of England Primary School, Isle of Wight; Cheddington Combined School,
Buckinghamshire; Dair House Independent School, Buckinghamshire; Deal Parochial
School, Kent; Glebe Infant School, Goucestershire; Henley Green Primary School,
Coventry; Lovelace Primary School, Surrey; Our Lady of Peace Junior School, Slough;
Tackley Church of England Primary School, Oxfordshire; and Twyford Church
of England School, Buckinghamshire for their invaluable help in the development
and trialling of the Bug Club resources.

Every effort has been made to contact copyright holders of material reproduced in
this book. Any omissions will be rectified in subsequent printings if notice is given to
the publishers.

2

Anya's Escape

Characters

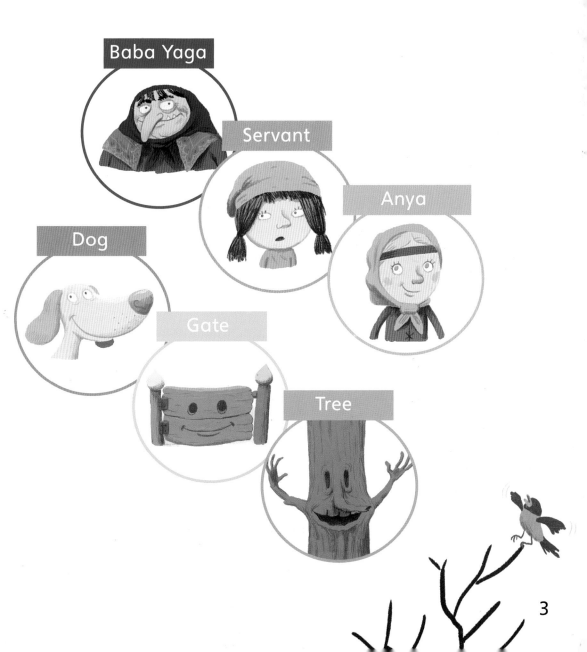

Baba Yaga

Servant

Anya

Dog

Gate

Tree

Baba Yaga: I've had nothing but potatoes to eat for months and months. I want something tastier!

Servant: I could make you a nice potato salad?

Baba Yaga: I'm a wicked witch. I can't eat salad, it's far too healthy!

Servant: A potato pizza?

Baba Yaga: Don't be ridiculous! What I really want is a lovely, delicious child.

Anya walks down the path to Baba Yaga's house.

Anya: I've been walking in this forest for hours and I'm lost. I wonder if this path here will take me home?

Tree: Here comes a child.

Gate: It's a girl!

Dog: She smells quite tasty!

Baba Yaga: Ooh, I smell her! My mouth is watering!

Anya: Oh look! A sweet little house. But how strange; it's standing on hen's legs.

Baba Yaga: Heat the oven, servant! I think I will roast her.

Servant: Right away!

7

Anya: Look at that tree! One of its branches is broken. Here, let me tie it up with my hair ribbon.

Tree: Oh! That's lovely!

Anya: There's a gate. I wonder if it's locked.

Gate: Come straight on through! Creaaak ... Ouch, I'm a bit rusty ...

Anya: I have some oil – let me put some on your hinges.

Gate: Ooh, that feels wonderful. I can't remember the last time I swung this easily!

Anya: Oh dear, is that a dog? He looks so thin – I hope he won't bite me! Here, have the leftovers of my lunch.

Dog: Chicken! Yum! It's been so long since I had any meat.

Baba Yaga: I think I'll boil the girl instead – that will be much quicker. Servant!

Servant: Yes, mistress?

Baba Yaga: Put a pot of water on the fire. Quickly!

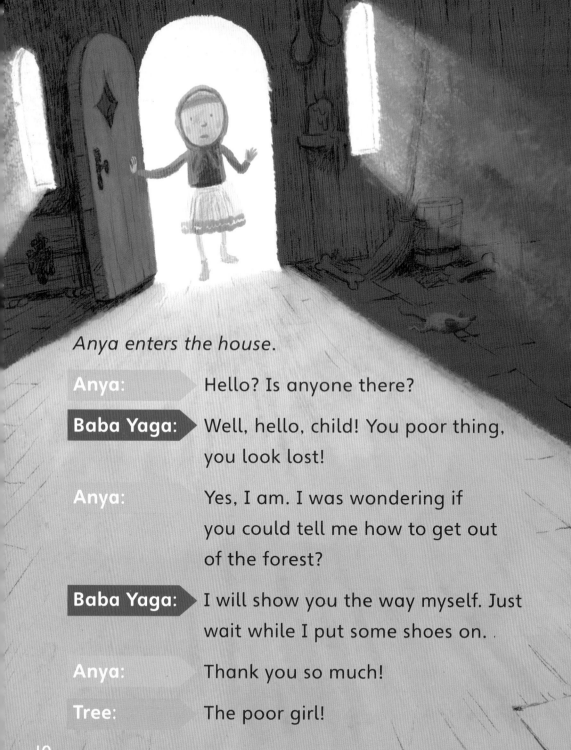

Anya enters the house.

Anya: Hello? Is anyone there?

Baba Yaga: Well, hello, child! You poor thing, you look lost!

Anya: Yes, I am. I was wondering if you could tell me how to get out of the forest?

Baba Yaga: I will show you the way myself. Just wait while I put some shoes on.

Anya: Thank you so much!

Tree: The poor girl!

Gate:	She doesn't know how much danger she is in.
Dog:	But **we** can't warn her, or the witch will punish us!
Servant:	Sniff! Aaaa-choo!
Anya:	Here, I have a hanky in my pocket. Take it!
Servant:	Oh, you are so kind ... Achoo! I'm sorry I've made it all snotty.
Anya:	You're welcome. Er ... You can keep the hanky.

Tree: I feel so sorry for the girl!

Gate: Do you think we should warn her?

Dog: Servant, you must say something!

Baba Yaga: Ooh, my tummy is rumbling! Now where are my knife and fork?

Baba Yaga exits and, quickly, the servant whispers to Anya.

Servant: My dear, you must get away!

Anya: Why?

Servant: The old lady is a witch! She is planning to eat you up!

Anya: Oh no! What shall I do?

Servant: Run! Go down the path and turn right at the bottom. Keep going, and you will get out of the forest.

Anya: Thank you! Goodbye! Oh no, the dog!

Dog: I won't bite you!

The gate swings open.

Gate: Run!

The tree lifts its branches.

Tree: Quickly!

Anya escapes.

Baba Yaga enters.

Baba Yaga: Oh! Where is she? She's run away! Servant, why didn't you stop her?

Servant: She gave me a hanky. All these years I have served you and you have never even given me a tissue to blow my nose.

The servant stomps out of the house.

Baba Yaga: Dog, why didn't you bite her?

Dog: She gave me some meat. All these years I have guarded your house and you have never even given me a dry bone!

Baba Yaga: Gate, why didn't you shut the girl in?

Gate: She oiled my hinges – you've never done that once!

Baba Yaga: Tree, why didn't you trip her up with your long branches?

Tree: You have never trimmed me, but she tied back my broken branch with her hair ribbon.

15

Baba Yaga: Where is my axe? I am going to chop down the tree and the gate, and put them both on the fire. Then I am going to boil the dog and the servant and eat them, no matter how horrible they taste!

Tree: Oh no!

Gate: Please don't!

Dog: I really wouldn't taste very nice. Quite bitter, in fact.

Servant: Oh look!

Tree: The house is running away!

Dog: With the witch still inside!

Servant: Good riddance!

Baba Yaga: Noooooo ... STOP!

Baba Yaga and the Enchanted Water

Characters

Luka

Katya

Uncle (of Luka and Katya)

Aunt (of Luka and Katya)

Baba Yaga:

Servant

Scene 1

Uncle is reading a letter. Baba Yaga and her servant listen outside the window.

Uncle: Oh no! My brother and his wife have died.

Aunt: Who will take care of Luka and Katya?

Uncle: This letter says they're coming here. We could adopt them. After all, we don't have anyone else to leave our gold to.

Aunt: They might get lost in the forest. Let's go and meet them halfway.

Uncle: Good idea! Let's take the gold with us, in case of thieves.

Aunt and Uncle exit.

Baba Yaga: Ooh, interesting ... Servant!

Servant: I'm here!

Baba Yaga: I'm going to steal that gold. But first we must be invisible. **Abracadabra**!

Servant: Oh no – I can see right through my stomach. I **hate** it when that happens!

Scene 2

In the forest.

Luka and Katya enter.

Luka:	I'm so thirsty!
Katya:	We'll be there soon.
Luka:	Look, a cow's hoof print full of water! I could drink that.

Katya: No! **Never** drink water from a hoof print. It's enchanted! You'll turn into the animal that made it.

Uncle and Aunt appear in the distance. Now invisible, Baba Yaga and her servant follow.

Uncle: Where are those children?

Aunt: I'm sure we'll find them soon.

The servant mutters to herself.

Servant: I really hate being invisible. I keep tripping over my feet!

Baba Yaga whispers to Luka, like a voice in his head.

Baba Yaga: Katya doesn't know everything, you know.

Luka mutters to himself.

Luka Look, a goat's hoof print. I bet it wouldn't really hurt to drink water from it ...

Luka drinks, and turns into a goat.

23

Katya: Luka, where are you?

Luka Meh!

Katya: A goat! Luka, is that you?

Luka Meh! Of course it's me!

Katya: You drank enchanted water, didn't you?

Luka Meh!

Katya: Oh, what's the point of talking to you? You're a goat.

Luka Can't you understand what I'm saying? Meh!

Katya: I can only hear bleating. What shall I do? If I tell anyone that you're enchanted, they'll be scared of you. They might kill you!

Uncle and Aunt approach.

Uncle: Katya!

Katya: Oh, hello, Uncle!

Aunt: Where's Luka?

Luka Meh!

Katya: Er ... it's just me and my goat. Luka died along with my parents.

Aunt: Oh, you poor child!

Uncle: You can come with us now, Katya.

Katya: Can my goat come too? I'm quite fond of it, even though it's rather stupid.

Luka Stupid? Meh!

Aunt: All right. It's a bit smelly, though!

Luka Hey, I've still got feelings! Meh!

Baba Yaga whispers to Katya, like a voice in her head.

Baba Yaga: You're a bit smelly too. Wouldn't it be lovely to bathe in that sparkling pool over there?

Katya: Uncle, may I take a quick dip? I feel so sticky!

Uncle: All right, but be quick.

Katya and Baba Yaga exit. Baba Yaga enters. She has made herself look like Katya.

Luka What's that turnip smell? Meh!

The servant whispers to Luka.

Servant: That's the witch. She imprisoned Katya in the enchanted pool and made herself look like Katya so she can steal your aunt and uncle's gold. Witches always smell of turnips. It's what gives them away.

Luka Can you understand me?

Servant: Of course, silly. I'm under an enchantment too, so I can see you're really a boy.

Luka We can't leave Katya trapped in the pool!

Luka and the servant run off.

Aunt: There goes your goat, Katya!

Baba Yaga: Actually, I'm not that bothered ...

Uncle: But we can't just let it escape!

Uncle and Aunt run off. They are followed by Baba Yaga, who still looks like Katya.

Baba Yaga: Come back! It's just a silly old goat!

Scene 3

At the pool.

Aunt: What's that in the water?

Uncle: Someone's in there! Let's pull them out ...

There is a splash.

Katya: Hello!

Aunt: It's Katya!

Baba Yaga turns back into herself.

Baba Yaga: You soaked me with enchanted water, you stupid girl!

Uncle: What's going on? You're an old woman! How come you looked like my niece?

Aunt: Look, the goat has turned into Luka!

Servant: The enchanted water splashed us all and reversed the other enchantments! I'm visible again! Hooray!

Uncle goes up to Baba Yaga.

Uncle: Someone has some explaining to do ...

Baba Yaga: It's time I was invisible again ... **Abracadabra**! Bye!

Servant: I suppose that means ... Yes, I'm invisible too. Thanks a bunch!

Luka is now a boy but he still bleats.

Luka I'm not a goat any more! Meh!

Katya: You look like Luka, but you still sound like a goat! Perhaps you didn't get much enchanted water on you. Oh well, at least I won't have to listen to your moaning any more …

Luka is furious.

Luka Meh!

Aunt: Come on, you two – let's go home.

Luka Meh!

32